JANE MARTIN, DOG DETECTIVE

BY EVE BUNTING

ILLUSTRATED BY AMY SCHWARTZ

A VOYAGER/HBJ BOOK

HARCOURT BRACE JOVANOVICH, PUBLISHERS

San Diego   New York   London

Designed by Vaughn Andrews

Printed and bound by South China Printing Company, Quarry Bay, Hong Kong

Library of Congress Cataloging in Publication Data

Bunting, Eve, 1928–
Jane Martin, dog detective.

Summary: A young girl solves three cases involving dogs.
[1. Mystery and detective stories. 2. Dogs — Fiction]
I. Schwartz, Amy, ill. II. Title.
PZ7.B91527Jan 1984   [E]   84-4497
ISBN 0-15-239587-3

A B C D E

JANE MARTIN,
DOG DETECTIVE

Jane pinned the poster on the pole. It said: HAVE YOU LOST A DOG? LET ME FIND IT FOR YOU. JANE MARTIN, DOG DETECTIVE. 23 OAK STREET. (MY TREE HOUSE IS AT THE BACK.) FEE: 25 CENTS A DAY.

Jane had made ten posters. This was the last one. Now she could go home and wait. Soon she would be a dog detective.

Jane did not have to wait long.

A boy yelled from under the tree. "Are you the dog detective?"

"Yes." Jane came down her tree ladder. She took out her notebook.

"I am Tim Wilson," the boy said. "My dog, Charlie, has been dognapped."

Jane wrote in her notebook: *Case number one — find Charlie, the dognapped dog.* "I will need to know everything," Jane said.

"Charlie was not in his doghouse this morning," Tim told her. "Someone left this note."

Jane read the note: *I have taken Charlie. If you give me one hundred dollars, you will get him back.*

"Hm," Jane said. "Who do you know who needs a hundred dollars?"

"Everybody," Tim said.

"Everybody is too many to watch. We will go to your house. You can show me a picture of Charlie. I will look for clues."

First Tim showed her Charlie's doghouse.

Jane tried to crawl inside. The doghouse was too small.

"I can see Charlie is not very big," Jane said.

"I can see *you* are a good detective," Tim said.

Jane nodded. "I can also see that Charlie is very tidy. There is no dish, no bone, no water."

"He is not always tidy. The dognapper took his dish and his bone and his hoop. He took Charlie's things so Charlie would be happy."

"Perhaps," Jane said. "Or perhaps there is a clue here. What does Charlie do with his hoop?"

"He can roll his hoop with his nose. Charlie is smart. He can even count. When I ask his age, he barks four times. Charlie always wins the Smartest Dog prize at the dog show. The show is next week. I hope you can find him by then."

Tim showed Jane a picture of his dog. Charlie was small and white and furry.

Jane tapped her head. "I am thinking. Someone wants to pretend Charlie is *his* dog. He will put Charlie in the show, and he will get the first prize."

"The prize is five dollars," Tim said.

"Who do you know who needs five dollars?"

"Everybody."

"Everybody is too many to watch. First we must see the list of the dogs that will be in the dog show."

The dog-show man was sorry that Charlie had been dog-napped. He showed them the names and kinds of dogs in the show.

"We can rule out some of these," Jane told him. "No one could make Charlie look like a German shepherd. Or a Great Dane. Or a sheep dog. Charlie is too small." She licked her pencil. "I need to check Patsy, Rover, Biff, and Flash. They are all small."

"You don't have to check Flash," Tim said. "I know him. He belongs to Susie. He is a very dumb dog. Do you know how dumb he is? He barks when there is no one at the door. When someone is there, Flash never barks. How is that for dumb? I wonder why Susie put *him* in the dog show."

"Hm," Jane said.

"The dognapper will not get away with this," Tim said. "The judges know Charlie. They will not be fooled."

Jane closed her notebook. "The dognapper may put dark glasses on Charlie. But I am a detective. That dognapper will not fool me. I will find Charlie. You go home now, Tim. Charlie may come back. Remember, he is a smart dog."

"Good luck," the dog-show man said.

Jane went first to the house where Patsy lived. But Patsy was a mother dog. She had ten puppies.

"You can't be Charlie," Jane said.

She went to Rover's house. Rover had long, long ears.

"You can't be Charlie," Jane said. "I don't think your ears grew since yesterday."

She went to Biff's house. Biff was *very* small.

"You can't be Charlie," Jane said.

She thought and thought. "Flash is the only dog left on my list," she said, "and Tim knows Flash. So Susie could not change Charlie for Flash. But why would Susie put such a dumb dog . . ." Jane stopped. "Aha!" she said. She felt like a real detective.

Jane ran to Flash's house. She rang the bell. A dog barked. Susie came to the door.

"Hi," Jane said. She showed Susie her dog detective card. "I want to see Flash."

"Why?" Susie asked.

"I am on a big case," Jane said.

"Flash! Flash!" Susie called. No dog came. "I will have to get him," Susie said. She came back with a little dog.

He didn't have new puppies. His ears were not too long. He wasn't too small. He could have been Charlie. But he was black. *Hm*, Jane thought. Susie could have dyed him.

Susie put the dog down. "Sit," she said. The dog lay down. "Up," Susie said. The dog rolled over.

"I can see that this is not Charlie," Jane said. "This dog is not very smart. He must be Flash."

But she knew that Susie had Charlie. She had worked it out in her detective brain. She still had to prove it. She remembered what Tim had told her.

"How old are you, Charlie?" she shouted very, very loudly.

From the back of the house came four barks.
Charlie had answered.
"The game is over," Jane told Susie. "Bring Charlie to me."
Susie looked scared. "How did you know?" she asked Jane.

"Why would you put a dumb dog in the dog show? It did not make sense. A detective checks when something doesn't make sense. When I rang the bell, a dog barked. Flash does not bark when someone comes to the door."

A small white dog ran into the room.

"Bark once if you are Charlie," Jane said.

The little dog barked.

"How did you get out?" Susie asked.

"He's a smart dog," Jane said.

Just then, someone rang the doorbell.

"Oh, dear," Susie said. "I hope that is not the police."

It was not the police. It was Tim.

He ran in when Susie opened the door. Charlie jumped into his arms.

"Oh, Charlie! Charlie!" Tim said. "I could not stay home," he told Jane. "So I went to Patsy's house, I went to Rover's house, I went to Biff's house, and then I came here. I heard Charlie bark. Why did you steal him, Susie?"

"I was going to give Charlie back. But first I wanted him to teach Flash his tricks. Flash does not like to be dumb." Susie bent to stroke Flash.

"That is why she took the hoop," Jane told Tim. "Charlie could use the hoop to teach Flash."

"I asked for a hundred dollars," Susie said. "It would take a long time for you to get a hundred dollars. It would give Flash time to learn. But I don't think he ever will. He is a very dumb dog."

"All dogs can learn," Tim said. "I could teach him." Tim was excited. "I will become a dog trainer. I will put up posters like Jane's. TIM WILSON, DOG TRAINER. 25 CENTS A WEEK. Do you want to hire me?"

"Yes, please," Susie said.

"Then I will not press charges," Tim said. "But you can pay the detective. Then you can pay me to teach Flash."

Jane opened her notebook. She wrote:

Charlie Wilson found, safe and smart as ever.
Case closed.
Signed, *Jane Martin, Dog Detective.*

JANE MARTIN, DOG DETECTIVE, AND THE KITTEN CASE

Jane Martin, dog detective, was in her tree house.
A boy yelled from under the tree. "Is the dog detective in?"
Jane looked down. A boy, a girl, and two dogs stood below.
The dogs were on leashes.

13

"I am the dog detective," Jane said. "My fee is twenty-five cents a day." She got her notebook and came down the tree ladder. "I find lost dogs. Your dogs seem to be here."

"This is not that kind of case," the boy said. "We need a *very* good detective."

"You have found her." Jane opened her notebook. "Tell me everything."

"Someone is telling lies about our dogs," the girl said. She patted her dog's head. "Spot is good. He would not do bad things."

"Mutt is good, too," the boy said.

"Who is saying these bad things?" Jane asked.

"Mrs. Nelson. She says one of them is chasing her cat, Kitten. Every night something chases Kitten up a tree. Every morning Mrs. Nelson has to go up and bring her down."

"Hm," Jane said. She wrote in her book: *Show that Spot and Mutt are good dogs. Find out who chases Kitten up that tree.* She looked at the boy and the girl. "Tell me your names, too."

The girl was Dot. Jane wrote: *Dot and Spot.*

The boy was Jeff. Jane wrote: *Jeff and Mutt.*

They told her they lived on the next street.

"I will start work right now," Jane said. "Show me the tree."

The big oak tree was in Mrs. Nelson's yard. There was a feather under the tree.

"Hm," Jane said. "A bird lives up there."

"You are a good detective," Jeff said.

A cat sat on Mrs. Nelson's porch.

"That is Kitten," Dot said.

The two dogs began to bark. Kitten stared at them. She did not move.

"Kitten is not scared of these dogs," Jane said. "These dogs would not make Kitten run up a tree."

"I will say it again," Jeff told Jane. "You are a good detective. But Mrs. Nelson thinks it is Mutt."

Mutt put his tail between his legs.

"We told her our dogs are not out at night," Dot said. "She says one of them has to be. It's because I live on one side of her —"

" — And I live on the other side." Jeff shook his head. "I told her it could be a dog from another street."

"Or another town," Jane added.

"She says she will call the police," Dot told Jane. "That's why we came to you."

Jane nodded. "These dogs are getting a bum rap."

"What's that?" Jeff asked.

"It is detective talk. It means they didn't do it. And I have an idea. Come to my tree house tomorrow. I may know then who is scaring Kitten."

That night, when it got dark, Jane went to work. She took a bag of her mother's flour. She put flour at the back door of Jeff's house. She put some at his front door.

She put flour at the back door of Dot's house. She put some at *her* front door.

As she stood up, she felt someone behind her. Jane jumped. "Who are you?" she whispered.

"I am your mother. I don't like you to be out alone after dark."

"But I am on a case," Jane said. "Detectives go out alone after dark. Detectives do *not* take their mothers."

"Sometimes a detective has a tail. A tail is someone who walks behind and watches."

"Hm," Jane said. "That is true. But a tail never speaks or butts in."

"That is true, too," her tail said.

Jane and her tail walked down the street. Dogs barked at them as they passed. Jane put flour at the doors of houses where dogs lived.

"Now we shall see," Jane told her tail. Her tail nodded.

The next morning, Jane got up early. She went back to all the houses where she had put flour. She checked the flour for pawprints. No dogs had come out in the night.

Jane saw a little kid open his door. "It snowed," he yelled.

Jane sighed. She was glad someone was happy.

When Dot and Jeff came, Jane said: "Both your dogs were in all night. I know that for sure because I am a detective."

"We know it, too," Dot said. "But who chased Kitten up the tree?"

"Was Kitten up the tree again last night?" Jane asked.

Dot nodded. "There was a loud scream . . . a bad scream. Mrs. Nelson rushed out. Poor Kitten was back in the tree."

"Hm," Jane said. "I will have to look some more. Come back tomorrow. I may know then who is scaring Kitten."

"I hope so," Jeff said. "This is costing us twenty-five cents a day."

That night, Jane got her bag of flour. She went out. Her tail went behind her.

"Hi," Jane said.

"Tails don't talk," her tail said.

Jane put flour around Mrs. Nelson's tree. Kitten watched from Mrs. Nelson's porch. Jane's tail watched from Mrs. Nelson's gate.

"I will take pawprints here," Jane told Kitten. "Then I will pawprint every dog in town. That way I will find out who is chasing you up this tree."

Kitten didn't answer.

Jane's tail didn't answer, either.

Jane went out early next morning.
She heard Kitten crying in the tree.
Jane felt angry. "Poor little Kitten. I will find who is doing this bad thing."

Jane checked the flour. "Aha!" she said. "Another feather from the bird. And something else. Paw-prints!" She looked closely. "This is a clue. These pawprints are very, very small."

Then she saw Kitten's little paws. They were white and dusty. "These are *your* pawprints, Kitten. No one was here but you. So what scared you? This is getting spooky."

Dot and Jeff were in the treehouse. Spot and Mutt waited below.

"Any luck?" Jeff asked.

Jane shook her head.

"And now we owe you fifty cents," Jeff said sadly.

"I have been thinking," Jane said. "A good detective thinks a lot. Now I have a new idea. But I need you both to help."

Dot clapped her hands. "Good. We want to help."

"Do *you* pay *us*?" Jeff asked.

"No. I am still the detective. Meet me after dark on Dot's porch," Jane said. "We will keep watch on the tree. Detectives call this a 'stakeout.'"

"It sounds good to eat," Jeff said.

"No. It's not that kind of steak."

That night, Jane got her flashlight. The tail got her flashlight, too. Jane did not tell the tail that she was glad to have her along. But she was. It was very dark outside.

Dot and Jeff were on Dot's porch.

"There is Kitten," Dot said.

Kitten lay in the long grass of Mrs. Nelson's yard.

Jane's tail stood on the sidewalk.

"Don't worry about that person," Jane told Dot and Jeff. "She is a sort-of detective. She is on the case, too."

Just then, Kitten stood up.

"I think Kitten is going after a mouse," Dot whispered.

"*Sh!*" Jane wasn't feeling very brave. What kind of thing had scared Kitten? What kind of thing left no pawprints? Or footprints? It had to be a spooky kind of thing. She was glad her tail was close by.

Something went *Whoo-ooooo.*

Something moved in the long grass.

"I don't want to see a mouse get eaten," Jeff said.

"Sh!"

There was a loud scream.

There was a *whoosh* of air.

Something flew past Jane's head.

Jeff yelped.

Dot squeaked.

Kitten cried.

"It's all right," Jane's tail said. "I am here."

Jane turned on her flashlight. Her hand shook. She saw Kitten going up a tree. In the air was something brown. Something with wings and big, yellow eyes. It flew away. A feather drifted down.

"It's an owl," Jane said. "Cats are out at night. So are owls. They both look for mice. There is an owl living in Mrs. Nelson's yard. It was the owl that screamed the bad scream. And those were owl feathers."

"I wasn't a bit scared," Jeff said.

"Yes, you were," Jane said. "I was, too."

A light went on in Mrs. Nelson's house. "Kitten?" she called. "Kitten?"

Jane marched to Mrs. Nelson's porch. "I am Jane Martin, dog detective," she said. "Here is my card."

Mrs. Nelson looked at the card. "What are you doing here?"

"I am working on the Kitten mystery," Jane said.

Mrs. Nelson looked at Dot and Jeff. "Where are your bad dogs? Chasing my Kitten?"

"The dogs are not doing that," Jane said. "May we come in?"

"Yes. But first, I must go up the tree for Kitten."

"I will get Kitten," Jeff said. And he did.

They all sat around Mrs. Nelson's table. The tail came, too.

Jane told Mrs. Nelson what had happened. "The owl screamed. It scared Kitten. She ran. It seemed safe in the tree. Tomorrow you will find an owl feather under the tree," Jane said. "That owl drops a lot of feathers."

"That is proof, Mrs. Nelson," Dot said.

Mrs. Nelson nodded. "Tomorrow I will tell Mutt and Spot that I am sorry. But what will I do about Kitten? I cannot make the owl go away."

"Kitten will have to share the yard. She will have to get used to the owl," Jane said.

Mrs. Nelson nodded again. "I think you are a very good detective, Jane Martin."

"Thank you," Jane said. "Please tell your friends. I need more cases."

She opened her notebook. She was tired. But a good detective takes time to write up her case. Jane wrote: *Kitten Case closed. The owl did it.*
Signed, *Jane Martin, Dog Detective.*

JANE MARTIN, DOG DETECTIVE, AND THE BOO-BOO CASE

The girl came to Jane Martin's tree house. Jane could see that she was sad.

"I know you are a good dog detective," the girl said. "I hope you can find my dog. He has been lost for two weeks."

"Two weeks!" Jane said. "That is a long time. Did you look in the animal shelter?"

"He is not there."

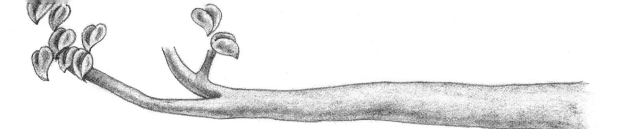

Jane opened her notebook. "I need to know your name. And the dog's name."

"I am Kay Walker. My dog is Boo-Boo. Look! I brought a picture of him."

"The picture will help," Jane said. Boo-Boo was a black poodle. He had a red collar.

"He has nice eyes," Jane said. "Does he have tags?"

"Yes," Kay said. "That is why I am scared. His name is on the tag. Where he lives is on it, too — 210 Brook Street. Every day Boo-Boo went out by himself. But he always came home. Two weeks ago he went out. And he did not come back."

"It is not good to let dogs run free," Jane said.

Kay's face got red. "I know. But he liked to go."

"Tell me some things about Boo-Boo," Jane said.

Kay thought. "He can beg. He can give his paw." She thought some more. "He loves ice cream. He loves to run after trucks."

Jane smiled. "He is a real dog!"

She wrote everything in her notebook. "Come to my tree house tomorrow," she told Kay. "Perhaps I will have Boo-Boo."

"I hope it will not cost too much," Kay said. "I only have five dollars."

"My fee is twenty-five cents a day." Jane closed her notebook. "Do not worry. I am a fast worker."

Kay took twenty-five cents from her pocket.

"I will go to work right away," Jane said.

They came down the tree ladder and shook hands.

First Jane checked all the kids on Brook Street. She showed them pictures of Boo-Boo. "Have you seen this dog?" she asked. It was hard work. It was the kind of work detectives must do.

Most of the kids knew Boo-Boo. "He runs down this street every day," one boy said. "He goes around that corner. But I have not seen him for a long time."

"Thank you." Jane went around the corner.

A lady was working in her yard. Jane showed her dog detective card. Then she showed Boo-Boo's picture.

"Boo-Boo passes here all the time," the lady said. "I think he goes into the park. But I have not seen him for a week or two."

"Thank you. Is the park close to here?" Jane asked.

The lady nodded. "It is two streets down."

Jane went to the park. A man sat on a horse near the park entrance. He was a policeman. Jane showed him Boo-Boo's picture.

"A lot of dogs come in here," he said. "They should not be in the park. But they are."

"Have you seen this one?"

The man shook his head. "Dogs all look the same to me."

"It is good that you are not a dog detective," Jane said.

Jane walked on all the paths. She was looking for clues. There was a bit of ice-cream cone on the grass. Jane picked it up. "No," she said, "this was not Boo-Boo's cone. Boo-Boo would have eaten all of it."

The cone gave her an idea.

There was a shop near the entrance. Jane got a dish of ice cream. It cost twenty-five cents. But to a good detective, money is not everything. Jane put the ice cream beside a lamp post. Dogs like lamp posts. And dogs are good smellers. Boo-Boo loved ice cream. He might smell this and come for it.

Flies came.

Ants came.

A white cat came.

A blue jay came and chased the cat.

A black dog came. It was not Boo-Boo.

Jane shooed them all away. The ice cream melted. A chipmunk came. Jane let him have the ice cream. She put the dish in the trash and went home.

Kay came the next day.

"No luck," Jane told her. "But I have a new idea. Boo-Boo went out every day. Did he always go at the same time?"

Kay nodded. "At three. He came back at four."

"Hm." Jane tapped her head. That helped her to think. "What happens at three every day?" she asked herself.

She answered herself: "Kids get out of school. This is summer. There is no school. But the time is a clue." She tapped her head again. "Come back tomorrow, Kay. I may have Boo-Boo."

"Here is your fee for today," Kay said.

Jane took the twenty-five cents. "Thank you. I gave a party with the last twenty-five cents."

"A party?"

"Never mind," Jane said. Good detectives keep secrets.

At three o'clock Jane started from Boo-Boo's house.

She walked as fast as a poodle would run. She walked along the street.

Around the corner.
Past the lady's yard.
Into the park.

It was an old detective trick. It was called "tracing the steps of the lost dog."

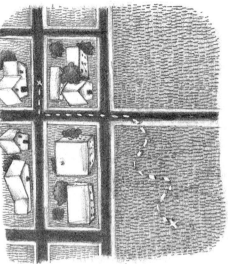

The mounted policeman smiled at her. "Have you found him yet?"

Jane shook her head. "No."

"I will keep an eye out," he told her.

"Thank you," Jane said. "Someday I will help you on a case."

She kept walking. This time she was looking for a *why*. Why did Boo-Boo come here each day at three? She hoped she would know the *why* when she saw it.

Then she *heard* it! Music! Happy music! And then she saw it! The *why* was an ice-cream truck. Of course! Boo-Boo had come to meet this truck each day.

The truck moved slowly. The happy tune played over and over.

Jane ran toward it. She held up her hand.

A man put his head out of the window. He was smiling. "What would you like?"

Jane showed him the picture. "Have you seen —" she started to ask. Then she stopped. A black poodle was on the seat beside the man. Its collar was blue, not red. There were no tags on the collar.

"Boo-Boo!" Jane said.

"Wuff!" The little dog wagged his tail.

The man was not smiling now. "This dog's name is not Boo-Boo. This dog is Fang. He is my dog."

"How long have you had him?" Jane asked.

"A while."

"Two weeks?" Jane asked.

"About that. He was a stray. He was living in the park. Each day he ran after my truck."

"Aha," Jane said.

"I gave him ice cream."

"Aha again," Jane said.

"He was no one's dog," the man told her. "So I took him. Each day now he rides with me. It is nice for both of us."

"This is Kay Walker's dog." Jane showed him her dog detective card. "I must take him. I have been working on the case for the past two days."

The man petted Boo-Boo. "That girl must not like her dog," he said. "She let him run wild. Dogs should not be in the park alone. I keep Fang on a long leash. He cannot jump out and get hurt."

"He cannot jump out and run home," Jane said. "If he could, he would."

"He would not. He loves me." The man looked sad.

Jane was sorry for him. "Why don't you get your own dog? You could go to the animal shelter. There are good dogs there. Any dog would like to ride with you. But this is Kay Walker's dog."

The man petted Boo-Boo. "He wants to stay with me."

"Take off the leash," Jane said. "We will see."

The man took a dish of ice cream from the freezer. He pulled off the lid. He put the dish on the seat beside Boo-Boo. "Here, Fang," he said. "Stay, Fang." He took the leash from the door handle. "Stay, Fang."

Boo-Boo cocked his head. He looked at the ice cream. He looked at the man. He looked at the open window. "Wuff!" he said. He jumped and was gone. His leash trailed behind him.

"I did not think that dog would say no to ice cream," the man said. "That dog must really love Kay Walker."

"You took off his tags, didn't you?" Jane asked. "That was bad. That makes it stealing. You knew he was Kay's dog."

"I did not. Kids in the park did it. They took the collars off a lot of dogs. They hung them on a tree. Look!"

Jane looked. Five collars hung on the tree. One was red with a silver tag.

"I did not try to find who owned Boo-Boo," the man said. "That was bad. But I wanted him very much."

"All is well that ends well," Jane said. "I will take that red collar home to Kay. I will bring your blue collar back. It will be for *your* dog. The one you get at the animal shelter."

The man gave her the dish of ice cream. Jane ate it as she walked. It was good ice cream. She could see why Boo-Boo chased this truck. Then Jane sat on a bench. She wrote in her notebook: *The ice-cream man did it.*
Boo-Boo Case closed.
Signed, *Jane Martin, Dog Detective.*